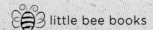

For Freddie, Madeleine and Ben—
with love, now and always.
And a big thank you to David.
L.S.

For George and Noah. x
D.T.

little bee books

An imprint of Bonnier Publishing Group
853 Broadway, New York, NY 10003
Text copyright © 2015 by Leilani Sparrow
Illustrations copyright © 2015 by Dan Taylor.
First published in Great Britain by Boxer Books Limited.
This little bee books edition, 2015.
Manufactured in China
First Edition 2 4 6 8 10 9 7 5 3 1
Library of Congress Control Number: 2014958645
ISBN 978-1-4998-0111-8

www.littlebeebooks.com
www.bonnierpublishing.com

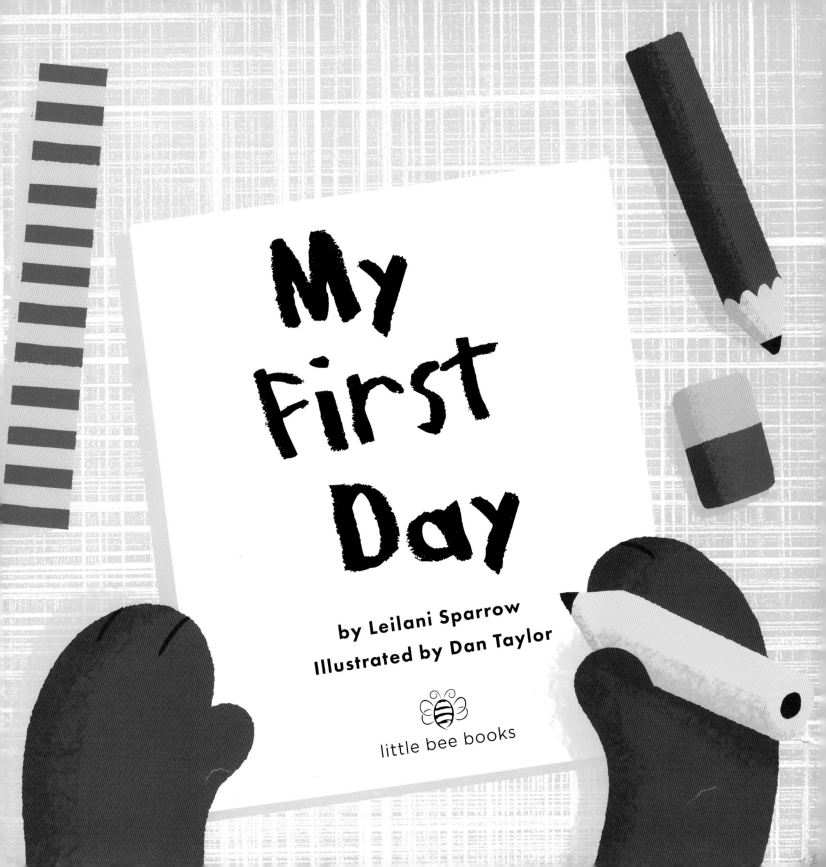

My First Day

by Leilani Sparrow

Illustrated by Dan Taylor

little bee books

Here's my hook.

It's my first day!

Here's a friend.

Come on,
let's play!

I sip my drink.

We share a snack.

I write a letter. . . .

What was that?

I paint a picture.

I take a tumble.

I have a boo-boo.

Then I grumble!

Now it's lunchtime.

We sit down to eat.

Won't you come and take a seat?

We share a story.

Then the bell goes . . .

DING! DING! DONG!

I grab my coat.

I have to run.

Tomorrow will be

so much fun!